THE
ADVENTURES
OF A

AUTHOR: VICTOR ALEX

TABLE OF CONTENT

CHAPTER ONE

THE BOY CALLED ALEX

A new story book was introduced to the pupils of Basic Four, by Mr John. Mr John wore a white shirt tucked in a blue trouser, while he waved the book at his pupils, who sat looking at their teacher.

"What is the title of this book?" asked Kelvin.

"Look at the front cover well, what is written on it," said Mr John.

"The poor boy and the rich girl", chorused every pupil. "That is good,give yourselves a round of applause commanded Mr John. Every pupil did as commanded, and Mr John beckoned on them to stop.

This is one of the story books we will read this term. I have a number of copies for all of you. When you get One, collect the money from your parents and bring them tomorrow. Is that clear?" "Yes, sir!" chorused every pupil in ecstasy.

Mr John shared the copies to every pupil after which he told them to open to Chapter One. He began to read while others followed. Soon, he stopped and asked:

"Who will continue from where I stopped?"

"I !!!" ,chorused everyone with their hands raised.

"Alex, come and stand before the class and read on". Alex came and stood before the class. He read fluently, and was encouraged by the class teacher.

After school, Alex got to the school gate and met His dad's driver was waiting in the car. "Come! Come in, Alex. Let me drive you home", said Johnson.

"Johnson, I want to trek home.

I don't want you to drive me home", replied Alex. "Ah!! Please, Alex, don't let me lose my job. Come in and let me drive you home. If your dad and mum get to know that you trekked home, they will get very mad at me and take my job from me", pleaded Johnson.

Johnson never knew how hard Alex had made up his mind, he opened the door, but Alex began to run.

"I want to trek home, my friends call me butter-boy, They say an egg is stronger than Ido. Johnson, go home with the car. I want to walk home", said Alex as he ran. Johnson alighted and ran after the so-called naughty Alex, and seeing that he couldn't catch him, he decided to go back to the car.

Alex passed through short corners and was about entering the street when he hit an egg hawker. She was carrying a tray containing six crates.

"Somebody, help me oh!!! shouted the egg hawker as she held the eight years old boy by his shirt. Alex threw his water-bottle up, and as the hawker looked up, her grip became a little loosened. Alex set himself free and ran dropping his school bag by the tray which laid on the ground

"Somebody, catch him! He is a thief, he's running", shouted the hawker as she pursued after the school boy. Passers-by watched to see how the matter would end, and in a jiffy, Alex bashed into the compound leaving the gate open. The gateman, who was sleeping on a mat beside the kennel, Jumped up. The hawker bashed in. As she ran, a big police dog ran after her.

"Somebody, help me!! This is my grave-yard", shouted the hawker, who ran round the house and ran out of the house

Daniel the gateman ran as fast as he could and stopped the dog from going out. While the egg howker ran like a mad woman to her home, Alex's bag laid on the ground at Kate Street, waiting for Alex to come and pick it.

QUESTIONS

1. What was introduced to pupils in Basic Four?

2. Who is the class teacher?

3. Why did Alex decide not to board the car?

4. What accident did Alex have on the way?

5. Who chased the egg seller out of the house?

CHAPTER TWO

THE TORTOISE AND THE SNAKE

Mum returned from her supermarket in the evening and saw that the house was smoky. She dropped her handbag and shopping-bag on the floor, and ran to the kitchen.

What is going on here? Where are Alex and Clara? Alex! Clara!", she called. Clara ran out from her room and went to embrace mum who was standing with arms akimbo, moving her eyes to and fro. "Clara, where is Alex? Why has smoke filled the whole apartment? asked mum impatiently.

"Mum! You are back, shouted Alex, who came out from the balcony. "Alex, the house is getting burnt. Where is the smoke coming from?" asked mum.

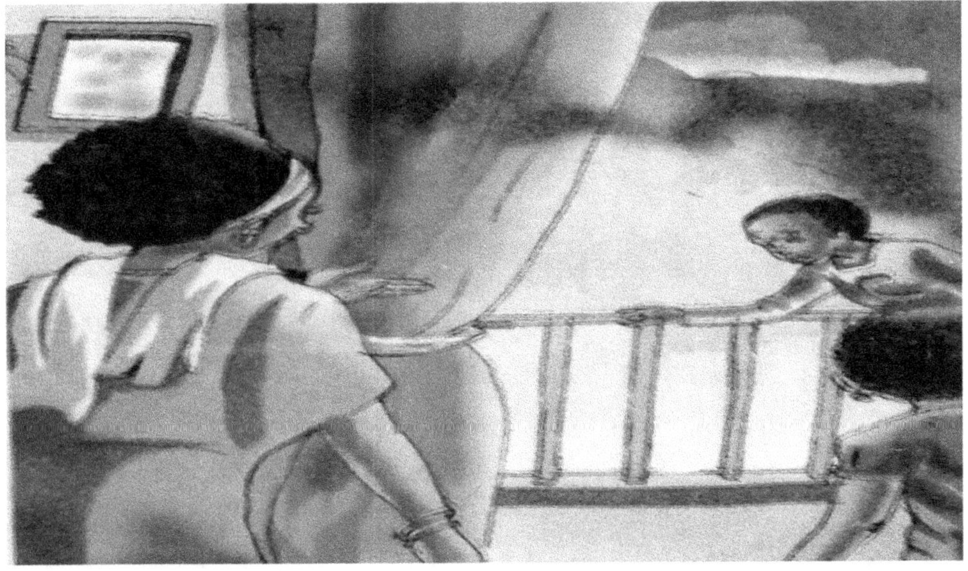

"Mum, I caught a bird on the balcony. I have made a fire there. I learnt that roasted birds are sweeter than boiled ones", said Alex with a broad smile. "You said what! Oh, Alex has killed me", screamed mum, as she ran to the balcony. She discovered the raw fire Chubi made with fire woods, and wondered on where he learnt how to make wood fire

"Oh God! Alex will kill us in this house", she said, as She removed the woods out one after the other. She used a big paper to pick up the burnt bird.

"Ouch! My hand", shouted mum.

"Sorry, mum!, " said Clara.

After cleaning up the place, she went in search of Alex. "Where are you, Alex? Alex boy!", she called, using the sweetest voice Alex only hears once in a blue moon. "Alex, come and have some snacks", she said, moving from one room to the other with a cane in her hand.

"Mum, Alex is in the toilet. He's hiding there" said Clara, Alex's younger sister

Mum went to the door side of the toilet and began to praise Alex. "My father! Alex, you know that you are my incarnate father, come out and have your snack. I have forgiven you, mum said enticingly. Alex, who has known his mum so well, began to moan.

"Hmn!!!Grrh!! ! I ..am.. coming. The feces is too strong", Alex stammered with fake words. He knew if he should come out, mum would pounce on him.

"Okay, I know what to do. If he says he is a tortoise, will tell him that I am a snake", mum thought. She held Clara by her left arm and went to the sitting room.

"Clara! she called. "Mum!", replied Clara. "Clara baby, I want you to go to the toilet's door, pretend as if you are eating ice cream, and lie to Alex that your dad is back. Will you do that for me?", said mum. "I will, mum, " agreed Clara. "That's my smart girl. Now, let us go". Mum and Clara returned to the toilet's door side, and mum kept calm.

"Alex, dad is back. I have with me your ice cream. Oh!! It's so delicious", said Clara.
"Clara, are you sure about what you just said?", asked Alex, from the inside. "Yes! You know, I don't tell lies. Open the door and have yours ``"Is mum at the door side "No, she is cooking in the kitchen".

"Okay!", Alex concluded, and opened the door. As he brought out his head, mum caught him by the shirt and dragged him out.

"W, a, p!!", the cane sounded on Alex's back. "Yeah!!! Mum, it's a mistake. I won't do it again", cried Alex as he struggled with the cane.

"Now you can see that a snake is wiser than a tortoise". "Yes, mum!". "w , a, p!!!" The cane sounded again.

QUESTIONS

1.

Who returned from shopping?

2.

Why was there smoke in the house?

3.

Why did Alex run into the toilet?

4.

Who acted like the tortoise?

5.

Who became the snake?

CHAPTER THREE

HOLIDAY IS NEAR

The third term examination drew nearer. Everyone in Basic Four class who knew what the promotion examination meant tightened their belts.

Alex was never scared of examinations. He was a good reader, and never toyed with the books. He had all the textbooks. His best subject was English. He I only managed to pass Mathematics. Although he had a home teacher, he never seemed to Complain about his difficulty in doing sums by himself.

"Don't worry, as you grow up, you will know more about how to deal with Mathematics", Alex's dad would

sometimes tell him. Alex was very bright but not all bright kids are good in mathematics.

The examination came and lasted one week and two days. On the day of the end-of-session party, Alex was given a gift as best dancer in a dancing competition. But in the area of position, he came fifth.

"Alex, you did not get a gift for a first, second or third position in your class, why did you take the fifth position?", said daddy "Dad, my class teacher made a mistake. Last term, I came fourth, and I'm supposed to be the second or even first this term because I worked harder", replied Alex, who sat on a sofa opposite his dad's seat in the sitting room."Don't mind the naughty boy. If you see the manner at which he danced at the party, you would call him Michael Jackson", mum chipped in. "Oh! That reminds me daddy! I won a gift as the best dancer in the school", Alex said excitedly. "That's not a good gift" said mum harshly. Don't mind your mum. That's nice! What is the gift?", asked daddy.

"Daddy, I thought it would be a toy car wrapped. But when I opened it, it was six sachets of indomie instant noodles. Chicken food!", said Alex with a snarl. Daddy laughed and asked; "where are the packs?" " I gave them to Clara. Clara is a chicken. She loves indomie. Dad, you know I love eating swallows", said Alex. "I'm not a chicken," said Clara.

"Don't mind the naughty boy, Clara baby", mummy sided Clara. "Dad, I came second in my class", said Clara. "Oh! That's my girl. Next term make sure you come first in your classroom, said daddy happily. "I will daddy. I am now promoted to Basic Three". Mum hugged Clara. "Daddy, look at my report card to confirm that my class teacher made a mistake. See, he wrote promoted to Basic Four instead of five", said Alex.

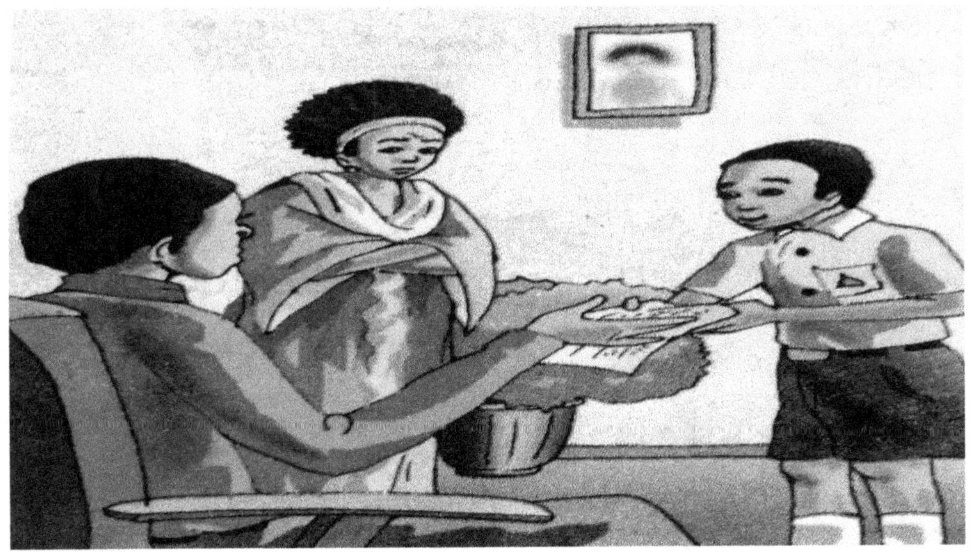

"Hmn!!! Alex! Darling, didn't you see a change on the card? That's Alex's writing", shouted mum.

"Oh, no!! It's not me. I didn't change it, my teacher, Mr John makes mistakes a lot. He even speaks like a teacher from the village"."Shut up, boy!. You don't talk about your teacher that way. That is his accent", mum said, as they busted into laughter.

"That reminds me. Clara and Alex will spend this long holiday in the home town. Grandma and Grandpa wants you both to come and keep them busy in the village", said daddy. "Wow!!! I love my home town. Dad, mum, remind me about the name of our hometown", said Alex. "Naughty boy, he does not even know the name of his home town", said mum mockingly. "Maya town in Lagos State. That is your home", replied daddy. "Maya, here we come", Alex said excitedly and ran into his room. "pray he doesn't get lost there", said mum.

QUESTIONS

1.

What drew nearer?

2.

Are all bright kids good at mathematics?

3.

What was Alex's position?

4.

Who altered a number in the report card?

5.

Where did dad say Alex would spend his holiday?

CHAPTER FOUR

THE HOMETOWN BOY

The arrival of Alex and Clara to the village brought so much joy to Grandpa and Grandma. As soon as Alex and Clara alighted from their dad's car, they flung themselves into the open and welcoming hands of their grandparents.

"Grandpa, your nose grew bigger", said Alex who was making investigations on the old fellow's looks. A loud laughter rented the air.

"Naughty boy, you don't say such to an old fellow", mum scolded him. "Oh, let the boy be. Let him say what he sees. I'm happy he's here again", said grandpa.``Let us go in, said grandma,

who would never let Clara go. Clara was as pretty as her grandma. Although grandma had now grown older than youthful beauty, you would know merely seeing her and Clara, that there was a time grandma, was looking so pretty like her pretty granddaughter.

"I have prepared a good meal for you all said grandma. "Grandma, I hope it is my favorite snail and vegetable soup", said Alex.

"Oh yes! How did you know? asked grandma.
"I know! You know I love that soup so well. Where is it
grandma? I am very hungry. My mum almost killed us with rice and chicken", said Alex. Mum raised an eyebrow while everyone laughed.

"I hope you will not behave naughtily. See village boys are far stronger than city boys. Once they notice that you are naughty, they would take you to the river, make you drink enough water and then take you to Agbala masquerade shrine where you would be sleeping and waking beside a horrible masquerade", said mum.

Fear ran across Alex's heart. He removed his gaze from his mum and landed it on grandpa.

"Grandpa, does such a thing exist here?" asked Alex
with a shaky voice.

"Don't mind your mum, she's joking", said grandpa. Mum went into the kitchen to help grandma. After the meal, friends and relatives came to welcome the city fellows. Mum gave them assorted biscuits, while a few elderly men were given one bottle of wine each by dad. One particular old man called Pa James, sat with grandpa as they drank loads of wine little by little, to their fill.

Daddy also drank alongside them, but he did not drink a lot. "Let them take their bath before going to bed", said grandpa. "I will bathe Alex and Clara myself", said grandma." The weather is cold, I won't take my bath", said Alex.

"You will, boy!" replied grandma with a smile revealing her three fallen teeth. "You can't bathe me Grandma, I am a big boy. I bathe myself in the city", said Alex. "Naughty boy!" said mummy. "You are still a kid, I will take good care of you", said grandma.

"No!!", Alex said and ran to stay with grandpa.

"Let him be. If that's what he wants, let him be".

"Yes, my grandpa says let me be, I'm a big boy".

Soon, everywhere got dark. Different sounds which became a noise that rented the environment. Clara could not withstand the noise of crickets and some other night creatures as she ran inside to sleep by her mum. Alex slept by his grandpa, snoring like one who had overworked during the day.

QUESTIONS

1.

Who is Clara?

2

Where is Alex's home town?

3

Do you know the name of your hometown?

4.

What was Alex's best soup?

5.

Who drank loads of wine?

CHAPTER FIVE

THE LOST BIRD HUNTER

Jackson is Alex's favorite relative living in the home town. He was a year older than Alex, and also proved to be far wiser than Alex when it comes to home town affairs. He often comes around to keep Alex's company.

Dad and mum spent two days in the village and left for the city. Alex had never spent more than one week in the village before, and that was during Christmas holidays. Now, they are going to stay for one month. While he moved about with Jackson, Jackson's sister, Mary, came around with her friends to keep Clara company. While Alex and Jackson carried out their adventures in the thick bush, Clara learnt new songs from Mary and other girl's play. In the evening, a few children gather round Grandpa to listen to stories. Grandpa was a good storyteller who often told children that he understood the languages of animals. Being an old man, everyone would believe him.

Alex knew it was impossible to hear the languages of animals and so waited for a day he would test his grandpa's knowledge.

One morning, two birds flew down from a palm tree before the house. Grandpa was seated beside the tree and Alex, who was coming out from the sitting room, saw the two birds playing.

"Grandpa, look at those birds, can you tell me what they are saying?" said Alex. Grandpa looked at him and smiled. He knew where Alex was going. "Well, Alex, old men don't tell lies to their children, so that their children and grandchildren won't become big liars. I do not know what the birds are saying.

All I can tell you is, it is only when I tell a story that I can mimic the voices of animals I talk about", said grandpa.
"Hmn!!! Grandpa!", Alex gasped
"Where are you going to ?" asked grandpa
"I am going to hunt birds with Jackson", replied Alex
"Where is Jackson?"
    "He should be at home. Grandpa, hasn't grandma and Clara returned from the farm? They are not yet back" Well, I am going. I won't stay long grandpa. Look at my bow and arrow. It's so strong. Grandpa, I brought home two birds yesterday, hope you enjoyed it. "Yes, I did. Jackson has taught you so much. Please be careful. Don't pick ripe fruits from people's farms. And when you see a masquerade, you run!"
"Okay, grandpa".
"Make sure you hunt down a big bird, a kite. I love kites".
"Okay, grandpa"
"Don't go far"
"Bye, grandpa!"
"Bye, grandson!"

Grandpa watched Alex walk merrily down the street. He shook his head, remembering when he used to hunt antelopes. "He's a city boy, he will never hunt such animals like me. His dad went to school, he also will, grandpa said and chewed a bit of kolanut.

Alex and Jackson met each other on the way, and Jackson told him that he was going to the stream to fetch some water alongside James and Patrick, his elder siblings. Won't you join us, the stream is not far from here", said Jackson. "When we get there, we will swim and have some fun in the stream", said James. "No, I don't like swimming, I just want to go and hunt birds. Will I be able to hunt birds at the stream side?" said Alex. "Yes, you will, come on, let we go", said Chima.

When they got to the stream, the boys fetched water into their containers, after which they decided to join other kids in swimming. "Water is sweet, come on, " Alex shouted at Jackson. "No, I won't. I want to go and hunt for birds at that side of the bush. I can hear the sounds of birds.

Oh! I can see them, they are many. I am coming, please wait for me", said Alex, as he ran into the bush holding enough stones in his pockets

"Today, I shall go home with so many birds. Let me make it fast", Alex soliloquized. As he went hunting, he came across a small hill in the center of the bush and noticed that birds stood on it in a relaxed mood. He moved closer in a cunning manner and was about to catch like two with his bare hands when the birds flew away. One of the birds entered into a hole in the ground, and as he looked into the hole, he saw the bird struggling. It is not a hole that his body can pass through only his hand. As he dipped his left hand into the hole, he felt the warm hand of an old man, who drew him into the hole. He saw himself in another world entirely.

1.

Who is Jackson?

2.

Is he older than Alex?

3.

Does grandpa really know about animal's languages?

4.

Where was Jackson going?

5.

Did Alex swim?

CHAPTER SIX

A NEW WORLD

"Here is the winner! the new great bird hunter of Dika kingdom. All hail the champion", shouted the old man while holding Alex's hand. A big cheerful noise rented the air Alex looked around, and saw many people clapping and hailing him. He looked at himself and discovered that the dress he wore had been exchanged. He was putting on a polo top and a jean trouser with nice footwear. But was surprised to see himself dressed in an attire he could not figure out how to describe. He was wearing a kind of nikka skirt, his chest and stomach were bare, and he had a necklace made of cowries hung on his neck.

"Sir, what is going on here? Please let me go, I do not belong here", he pleaded.

The old man did not listen to him. He tried to free himself from the old man's grip, and was surprised that the old man did not let him go. The man beckoned on everyone and a brief silence prevailed. Alex's eyes went to the man's head, and he discovered that the man had a crown on his head.

"Look at that cage everyone, this boy, our new hero whose name is Dike, caught those mighty birds", said the man as the hailing came into the air again, followed by another silence.

"Sir, I'm not Dike, I am Alex. Please let me go. My grandparents will soon begin to look for me", Alex pleaded. All his pleas landed on deaf ears.

Soon, he was set before a big mat where men of big calibers sat and food was served. Alex saw himself among them and kept calm.

"Dike, eat your food. Look at those big chicken laps, bird laps and tortoise necks, they are all for you. Taste it, you will like it", said the old man who sat not far from Alex. Alex stood and tried to run, but was stopped by guards who were twice taller than his father.

"This is your new home. It is better you take it or never dream or go back from here", said one guard.

"This is the only world you can think of. The earlier you adapt the better for you. You better eat before the king gets angry and throws you into the lion's den which is at the back of the palace", said another guard. Fear gripped poor Alex. He thought he was dreaming, and after he had forced and wished he had woken up, he got to realize that all that was happening to him was real.

"Where is Clara, where are my grandpa and grandma? Where is Jackson? Won't I see my parents again?" as he thought, a voice came stentoriously." Take Agu to the lion's den, since he has refused to eat my food" said the king. "I told you", said the second guard.

"Please, please king, let me be", screamed Alex."In this world, you don't beg an angry king", said guard one, who carried Alex like a bundled firewood. Soon, they arrived at the lion's den, Alex was thrown down amidst tears.

"Goodbye bird hunter, we will meet at God's kingdom, " said guard one.

As Alex turned, he heard the roar of a lion. "God help me!!! Ahhh...." he screamed.

As the lion drew nearer to catch him, he heard a stout voice "Jump! Jump! Jump!" Alex did not hesitate. He obeyed, and jumped, he soon found himself in the sky.

QUESTIONS

1.

Who drew Alex's hand?

2.

The old man was a?

3.

Why was Alex celebrated?

4.

What name was given to Alex?

5.

Why was Alex thrown into the lions' den?

CHAPTER SEVEN

THE DWARF OF EMILIO ROCK

Alex landed on a large rock whose surroundings are filled with both small and large rocks. As he landed, he began to fidget. He put his hand on his stomach and began to cry.

"I am hungry. I want to eat. Mum, where are you? Dad, where are you? Somebody, help me. I miss my grandma's snail soup. I am hungry", he said.

A neatly prepared food appeared before the poor boy, as he sat quietly and began to eat. It was his favorite meal, snail soup and pounded yam. After eating, he laid down and slept off in a jiffy.

By the time he went out to look. around, he saw that the apartment whose items were made of pure gold was built in a large rock" So, I haven't left this rock. Where am I? Who kept me in that apartment", said Alex who became afraid of going in again. He touched his stomach and felt its hardness.

"Oh, I overate, " he muttered. He heard some footsteps and was surprised to see the rocks shaking

"Gbim Gbim! Gbim!", the footsteps of Alex began to fidget. He began to look for where to run to for safety but found none. He then decided on going back into the pretty apartment.

"Oh, no! The door is shut. Who shut the door? The whole world is shaking", he said, flabbergasted. In no time, a man who proved to be the owner of the footstep got to the spot where Alex laid.

"Peter! Peter, my son! So, you are awake. I carried and put you on my golden bed. Sorry, I returned late", said the man. Alex looked at the man with great surprise and shook his head.

"This is a dwarf, how can this dwarf say he is my father? No, he's not", Alex thought. "I hope you had a Nice rest, Peter? Sir, I am not Peter, I am Alex. I am not your son. I don't know how I got here", Alex said and began to cry. "What! You are not my son, then, you are my slave. You are definitely Smith, my runaway slave. And you will work here as a slave till you grow old. it is only after you have grown old that I will let you go", said the dwarf, who began to laugh hysterically.

"Please, sir, I am not a slave. I am the son of Michael Mathew, a rich business man. I am not a slave", he pleaded. The dwarf hissed and made a snap sound with his fingers. A very big giant came out from a cave not far from them, and stood before the dwarf. "Take this slave, Smith to the cave of the merciless baboons", ordered the dwarf.

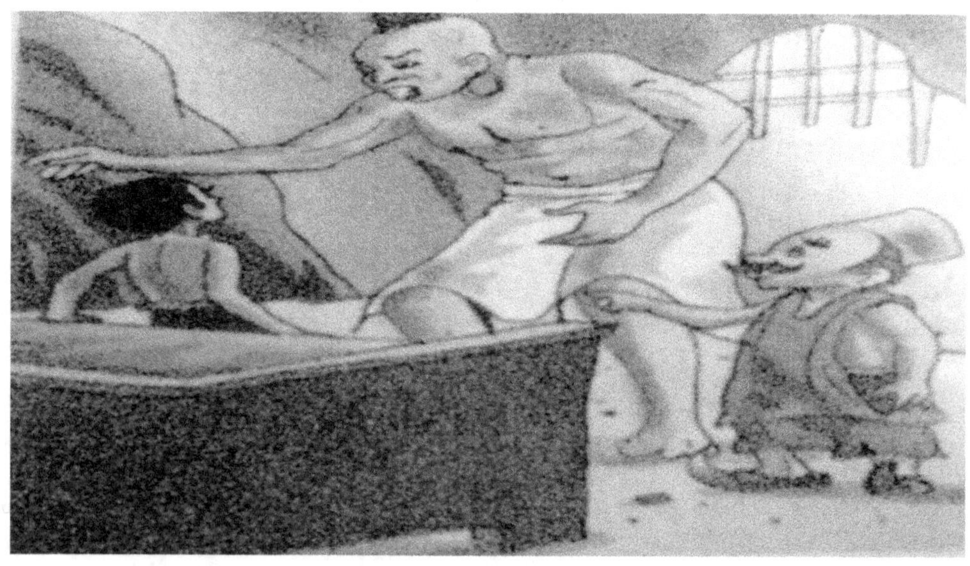

"Please let me go, I miss my parents, let me go...
The giant carried Alex like a cat and was opening the
gate to the cave when his attention was divided by a
whistle sound heard from a distance. The door flung
open, and the baboons came battling with the giant.
Fear gripped Alex. He had never seen baboons
except in a book on animal kingdom which he had at
home. The baboons defeated the giant and ran
away. Only one of the baboons came to him and
shook his hand.

"Thank you for saving us. Now, climb on my back,
I will help you too. Climb, and don't be afraid", said
the baboon. Alex looked back and saw the dwarf
coming. He climbed on the baboon's back, and the
The baboon ran like a whirlwind.

QUESTIONS

1

Where did Alex land?

2

Did he see anyone on the rock at first?

3.

What did he wish for?

4.

Who came to him?

5

Who was ordered to arrest Alex?

CHAPTER EIGHT

ALEX AND THE BABOONS

As the baboon journeyed with Alex on his back, Alex wondered how the baboon could speak the human language. "How did you learn man's language?" he asked. "Well, my name is Pitoo. I am five hundred and six years old", said Pitoo the baboon. "What! Incredible. How can you be five hundred years old?", asked Alex.

"You won't understand. I was formerly a man. But when I came to this world, I became a baboon". "What! How did that happen?" "The dwarf cast a spell on me and others. Thank your creator that he did not do so to you, you would have ended up as a baboon too". "God forbid!"

"Don't worry, you have helped me. I will also help you"."Thank you, Pitoo!" "Don't worry, friend. Let me take you to my brothers in the forest", They journeyed through the forest and finally got to their destination. The area was glittering. Other baboons waited for Pitoo to join them.

"Welcome, Pitoo!" said others in a chorus.

"Thank you, pals. Well, this is my new friend, Our savior. He will be our king now. We shall defend him with all our might. We must live in unity so that we won't fall prey again to the powerful dwarf of Emilio rock. All hail our king, king Mark of the baboons" said Pitoo.

"Long live our king!Long live our saviour.Long live king Mark", chanted other baboons. Alex could not say no to the baboons. He saw how friendly they were, and never rejected being their king so that he wouldn't fall into trouble with the baboons since he always fell into trouble through disagreement and unwillingness to yield. He noticed how wise he had suddenly became, and began to think of ways he could go back to meet his real family.

One morning, he called Pitoo and began to tell him about his former world."Please, Pitoo, you promised to help me.I want to go and say hi to my first family, but I do not know how to go about it. Please, help me", he said. "You mean you want to leave us here?" asked Pitoo. "No! no! no, I just want to go and say hi, I will return'", he lied.

"Okay, I will help you. But for us to help you go back, you will have to look for a hole on a hill where birds also play in this forest". "Won't you help me find it?" asked Alex. "I will, king Mark. But we will have to conquer the Wise tree-man"."Who is this wise tree-man? "He is a tall and hefty fellow whose body looks like a tree. His feet are made of roots. He is the wisest creature in this forest.

"Okay, I will go and see him. But how do we defeat him? Is it by fighting or what "No! no! no! no one can fight the tree-man. You will prepare your brain for an intellectual contest.

There is a hill at the back of his house, and birds gather there a lot. If we can defeat him, you will have your
way".

"Is that all?" Yes!"

"Okay, then, we will be there right away. Let us go", said Alex decisively. "I'm with you, my king", said Pitoo.

QUESTIONS

1.

Who were set free

2.

Who.helped Alex escape?

3.

Alex was made?

4.

His new name was?

5.

Why did Pitoo help king Mark?

CHAPTER NINE

THE WISE TREE-MAN

Pitoo carried Alex on his back as they embarked on the long journey to see the wise tree-man. On getting there, they saw a man whose physique resembled that of a tree. His head was long with a broad face. The hairs on his head were leaves. His hands were made of stems while his feet were made of roots.

The man was sitting before his house, a huge tree which had a door as its entrance. But the tree-man sat on a bench. Immediately the man saw king Mark and Pittoo, he stood up, yawned and bowed in greeting.

"I greet you, king Mark. What brings you to my house?" said the man. Thank you, Mr tree-man. But haven't seen you before, how did you get to know my name replied king Mark.

"Don't worry, before you were, I was", replied the tree-man sharply."Tree-man, please allow me pass through your house to the hill of Caban. I have an important matter to attend to", the king spoke like a king.

The tree-man chuckled and giggled. He then cleared his throat with a sharp but rough cough.

"I have just three questions to ask you, if you answer me correctly, you are free to go but if you fail, you will have to go back or a mighty wind will come and carry you to another world", said the tree-man.

King Mark's heart skipped. He gazed at Pitoo, who frowned trying to tell the king to forfeit the mission.

"Okay, let me hear the questions' ', said King Mark boldly. "There is something, when you cut me you cry, what am I? "I think it's onions. It's onions!" replied the king sharply. "Hmn! Well, the second is; tell me the meaning of this proverb; Wisdom is better than strength". "That means, it is better to use one's head than power most times' '.Fantastic! The third question is; Is an old man born old by his mother?" the tree-man asked and relaxed, expecting king Mark to fail. King Mark laughed and tapped Pittoo with his little golden stick.

"Tree-man, an old man is not born old. At first, he was born as a baby. He grows into a child, youth and adult,

before becoming an old man".

As soon as he gave the third answer, the door opened and Pitoo jumped excitedly. "You got them all! My king, you won", shouted Pitoo. "You can go in", said the tree-man. Pitoo and king Mark went in and soon saw themselves close to the hill of Caban.

"Look, those lovely birds are playing on the hill of Caban", said king Mark quietly. "Don't make noise. Just go nearer, there is a hole in the middle of the hill. Try to catch one and put your hand into the hole, you will see something new. But king Mark, I will miss you a lot.I will wait here and watch you do the right thing. Bye, king Mark", said the baboon, as king Mark hugged him.

King Mark bade him bye and forged ahead. As soon as he got nearer, he saw a new catapult in his hand, shot at a bird which fell into the hole. Other birds flew away, and as he dipped his left hand into the small hole, he felt another hand draw him out and he saw himself in the human world, the real world. He held the bird he caught, now putting on the original cloth he wore on the first day to the stream.

As he approached the stream, he heard mama Jackson call "Alex is that really you? Where have you been for the past three days? Oh Alex she hugged him and took him home.

1.

Describe the tree-man.

2.

Who took Alex to the tree-man?

3.

State the questions the tree-man asked.

4 .

State the answers to the questions.

5 .

Did Alex pass the test?

CHAPTER TEN

HOME AGAIN

Jackson's mother held Alex home, while Alex held a big bird he caught in the bush. The woman asked Alex so many questions, and all Alex told her looked like a mere story to her

"We will soon be at your grandpa's house. Everybody has been worried. Even your grandma refused to eat", said Jackson's mother."Really!"

"Yes! Your grandpa drank only alcoholic wine and would not taste food". "How about Clara,
Jackson and...." "Clara is also sad. Jackson and your older relatives have searched for you everywhere. They even Suggested that you had drowned in the stream".

"No, I didn't. I couldn't swim. They asked me to swim but refused. I went hunting in the bush"

Soon, they arrived home. Grandma was very happy, she ran to embrace her lost grandson who had last been seen three days ago. Why did you behave like this? Where did you go to ask grandpa and hit Alex with his walking stick?

"Grandpa, I lost my way", shouted Alex who ran to hide behind his grandma. Clara was happy to see Alex and also Jackson. As they were all rejoicing over Alex's return, a car drove into the compound. Mum opened the door and jumped out. "Grandpa, grandma have you seen Alex?" she asked fearfully.

"Yes, we have. Look at him, naughty boy", replied grandma. Daddy alighted from the car and went to greet his parents.

"Papa, we were so scared when we learnt that Alex had been missing. Now that he's back, we have come to take them back to the city", said mum.

"I am not going to the city now. I want to stay a little longer in the village", said Alex.

"Shut up! You want to put us in more trouble", shouted mum.

"Take it easy with the boy. He's not that bad. He loves hunting, farming, he's a farm boy", said grandpa.

"Papa, I'm so sorry, Alex will go with us tomorrow morning. He is my son and I know what he can do", said daddy.

The following day, mum, daddy, Clara and Alex got ready to go. Alex, who had devised a plan on how to stay a little longer, went and hid in grandpa's barn.

Mum, dad and grandma began to look for Alex. "Alex, where are you? If I should get you, I will make sure I cut off your two years. Since you have ears and
have refused to use them to hear, I will take them both and leave you earless", said mum angrily. They searched everywhere, including Jackson's house, until Jackson came around.

"Whenever I play hide and seek with Alex, he hides in one place you have not searched", Jackson.

"Where is the place?" asked mum and daddy one after another. "The barn! Grandpa's barn!" said Jackson. "Let us go", said mummy. As Alex noticed that his mum was approaching with Jackson, he began to make scary sounds which he learnt from the baboons. Mum got scared. She refused to enter the barn."Let us go in ma, it is Alex that is making that noise", said Jackson. "No, that's not Alex. That sound looks like the sound from a wild animal", said mum fearfully.

"Okay, watch me. I know Alex well, I will drag him out"

"Don't go in there, please I do not want you to get killed", pleaded mum. Jackson boldly went in and dragged Alex out. It was not a small struggle, but his bones were stronger than that of Chubi.

"So, you are the one making the sound of a wild beast. I will deal with you today", said mum as she held Alex tightly. After giving Alex some slaps on the back and a few pinches, she opened the door to the car and threw him in. "Take it easy with the little boy", said grandpa.

"I know him well, papa. Please, papa, allow me to train him well. Your bones are weak to do so again", mum concluded and entered the car. Dad gave some money to his parents and zoomed off.

"Bye, grandpa! Bye,grandma!" shouted Alex. Bye, farm boy!" shouted grandpa in ecstasy.

QUESTIONS

1.

Who discovered the lost bird hunter?

2.

Where was he seen?

3.

Why was everyone troubled?

4.

Where did Alex go to hide?

5.

Why did mum refuse to enter the barn?

NEW WORDS

Applause: To clap with two hands.

Beckon: To use hand in making signals either to come or stop.

Encourage: To help one who is distressed ina positive way.

Hawker: One who sells goods carried on the head or hand, about

Grip: Strong hold on something.

Naughty: To act in an amusing manner

Impatiently: An act of not being patient.

Relatives: People related by blood, e.g. cousins, nephews, etc.

Affairs: What one does either immediate or ona daily basis.

Baboon: Awild animal, which looks like a man, monkey.

Embrace: To hug or to hold tightly with affection.